My Dinosaur Sat on My Shiitake

Author: Stacey Murphy

Illustrator: Eileen Schaeffer

DEDICATION

This book is dedicated to that special someone
who notices magic all around...
you know who you are.

* * * * *

And a very special dedication to:

Stasha Washburn
Kimberly O'Brien
Debbie Carter
Will Condon
E.G.O.P. Ehrlinspiel
Tom Schaeffer

Thank you for believing that Eileen and I could pull
this dinosaur out of our hat. We are ever grateful for
this opportunity to inspire the next generation of
nature lovers.

* * * * *

ISBN: 1540857190
ISBN-13: 978-1540857194

CONTENTS

Stacey Murphy

ACKNOWLEDGMENTS

Thanks to all our Kickstarter supporters!
Because of you, the adventures of Nya and Bronty continue...

Stasha Washburn
Kimberly O'Brien
Debbie Carter
Will Condon
E.G.O.P. Ehrlinspiel
Tom Schaeffer
Mary Marchetti
Betty Marchetti
Chris Marchetti
Ed & Dorothy Segowski
Linda Patterson
Nathan
Ellen Rubenstein Chelmis
Michael, Teresa, Anna &
Maddy Marchetti
Liz Verity
Paula Tucker
Jon Clayshute
Laurie Niles
Joyce Kuik
Lisa Schropp
Farmstead Foodscapes
Elisa Smith
Aunt Jeanne
Matt Mathias
Rob & Katherine McAlister
Katherine Morgan
Howick Family
Martha Greenhow
Moonsprouts LLC
Victoria Marchetti
Regina King

Julia Snyder
Hila
J Spears, Star Patch Farm
Andrew Brantley
Ken Smith
Glenn Herbert & Karen Ellis
Jennifer Westerholm
Louis Marchetti
Molly Culver
Anjali Pingle
Thayer Porter
Nathan Alongi
Annie & Charley
Jim Cullen
Shelby Koebley
Charlene Eyles
Corey Pine Shane
Tandy Nicholson
Murphy
Hillary King
Jenna Henderson
Yane Brown
Aidan Johnson
Jeremy Reed
Grace L. Webster
Danielle Gould
Jeremy Smith
Patty Ghertner
Benasaurus Bruckman
Maureen Kelly-Dagle
Raina Chamberlain
Quinn Asteak

CHAPTER 1: SMASHED SHIITAKES

CRASH!

"Oops," cried Bronty. "My chair has crumbled to pieces!"

"That wasn't a chair, Bronty! You sat on my shiitakes!" laughed Nya.

"Oh no!" said Bronty. "Liam Lizard was growing them for the big celebration and now I have ruined them."

"Don't you worry your long neck about it," said Liam.

"In just seven days a shiitake will swell from a tiny spore seed into a mushroom!"

Bronty still looked a little sad.

"Tell you what," said Liam, "I'll grow more shiitakes for the big celebration and you two check in on Paulina. I don't think she's feeling well."

"Oh!" said Bronty, "I bet I can make her feel better. My GrannySaurus taught me all about the healing powers of plants!"

CHAPTER 2: SEVEN DAYS TO GO

Nya followed Bronty through the forest, looking for Paulina.

They stopped at a clearing when they heard a terrible groan.

"Oh!" cried Paulina PachyRhinoSaurus, her face pouring with perspiration. "Thank goodness you're here! I have a sore tummy and my temperature is very high!"

"Don't worry, Paulina," said Nya, stroking her friend's huge head. "Bronty's GrannySaurus taught him all about herbs. He'll whip up some medicine to make you feel better."

"It's true," said Bronty. "I'll brew up a bath and steep some tea. Peppermint and Yarrow have been used by our dino ancestors for ages to break a fever, ease the pain and soothe the tummy."

Paulina stepped into her healing bath and drank a nice cup of Peppermint tea.

"Oh, thank you!" she said. "I'm beginning to feel better for the big celebration!"

CHAPTER 3: SIX DAYS TO GO

"Hello, Nya. Hello, Bronty," yawned a very small voice from the bushes.

"Delia!" said Nya. "You're looking a little pale today. Are you okay?"

"My doctor said I might be anemic," Delia Dung Beetle yawned again. "So I need to add more iron in my diet to keep me strong."

"You're in luck Delia!" Bronty exclaimed.

"You're lying on Stinging Nettles which are packed full of minerals, including iron."

"Stinging nettles?" Ms Bee Bumble asked from nearby. "Plants can sting too?"

"Not if you're wearing gloves when you pick them," Bronty giggled.

"Or have a hard shell like me!" exclaimed Delia.

"Sauté these greens to remove that sting and eat up!" Bronty instructed.

"And once you're strong again, we'll see you at the celebration!" Nya waved goodbye.

CHAPTER 4: FIVE DAYS TO GO

COUGH!!

"What was that loud noise, Nya?" asked Bronty.

Nya and Bronty followed the noise to find a very ill looking Paul Parasaurolophus.

"Hello friends," mumbled Paul. "Don't come too close! I have the beginnings of the flu!"

"I'm afraid it's going around," said Nya. "But I'm sure Bronty will have something to make you better in time for the big celebration."

"Yes!" said Bronty. "GrannySaurus always said Elderberry syrup is perfect for flu. It's antiviral and very tasty too! For you Nya, a spoonful would do. Paul's a big dinosaur, so he'll need a lot more to feel well again."

Nya cooked up a river of syrup from the abundant Elderberries.

"Thanks! I'll drink this up and see you at the big celebration," Paul said.

CHAPTER 5: FOUR DAYS TO GO

"The Cold Forest is a short cut to the big celebration," Bronty steered Nya.

"But what if we get sick?!" she asked.

Bronty wasn't worried. GrannySaurus taught him well. "All we need is some Vitamin C to boost our immune system."

"It's much too cold for oranges," Nya thought aloud. "Where else can we find Vitamin C?"

Bronty lifted Nya on his nose high into the pine trees. "Grab the bright green tips of the Pine Needles," he instructed. "They are tasty and full of Vitamin C!"

Nya accidentally pulled some brown pine needles which jumped to life in her hands.

"Hey!" cried Portia Porcupine awaking from a nap. "Don't eat ME!"

"Oops!" Nya exclaimed as everyone laughed. "I got it now, just the bright green tips"

As they left, Bronty yelled back to Portia, "Come to the celebration. Everyone is invited!"

CHAPTER 6: THREE DAYS TO GO

Leaving The Cold Forest, Nya and Bronty ran into Ollie OviRaptorosaur.

He was nervously pacing in front of his house.

"Oh, friends!" cried Ollie. "I'm so scared about going to a new school. I don't know anybody there, and what if the teacher is mean?"

"Don't worry," reassured Nya. "It's always a little scary to do something new, but soon you'll make new friends."

Bronty noticed his favorite herb growing in the corner of Mommy OviRaptorosaur's garden.

"Here Ollie," he said. "I chopped up some Tulsi Basil into this delicious pesto for you. Not only is Tulsi Basil tasty, it helps you adjust to new situations."

Nya offered a tray to Ollie, "I brewed you some Tulsi tea, too."

"Mmmm," Ollie enjoyed the tasty treats of Tulsi pesto and tea.

CHAPTER 7: TWO DAYS TO GO

Nya and Bronty were waving goodbye to Ollie when...

"OUCH! I've been stung!" cried Nya.

A tiny voice sobbed, "I'm so sorry! It was an accident. You scared me."

It was Ms. Bee Bumble, the cutest little honeybee.

"You startled me too, Ms Bee!" Nya yelped.

"Don't worry," Bronty said. "There's Plaintain everywhere."

He chewed a great big mouthful of it and spit it on Nya's arm.

"Ewww! Why did you spit leaves on me, Bronty?" Nya wondered aloud.

"It's called a spit poultice," said Bronty. "It will draw out the sting."

Nya thought this was very funny, but her sting felt much better and there was hardly any swelling.

"Let's keep walking," Nya said. "I don't want to be late for the celebration."

CHAPTER 8: TWENTY-FOUR HOURS TO GO

"Hello you two!" shouted a booming voice. It was Angie Ankylosaurus.

Nya thought Angie look a little under the weather.

"Angie!" cried Nya. "You look very tired!"

"Yes," replied Angie. "I just can't sleep! I'm much too excited for the big celebration."

"We're all very excited," said Bronty. "But sleep is very important. When we sleep our brains develop and our bodies grow strong and healthy."

Nya suddenly realized, "Oh! So dinosaurs and children must need lots of sleep to do lots of growing!"

Bronty looked around for some plants to help Angie sleep.

"Here Angie," he said soothingly, passing her a nice cup of delicious tea. "This Passion Flower and Chamomile tea will have you asleep in no time."

"Oh, thank... zzzzz," Angie fell asleep mid sentence.

CHAPTER 9: EIGHTEEN HOURS TO GO

Nya and Bronty left Angie snoring loudly under the Passion Fruit trees.

"Look at all these weeds, Bronty!" observed Nya, seeing Dandelions dotted across the field.

"Harumph," snorted all the Dandelions together. "We're not weeds!"

"That's right," Bronty agreed. "My GrannySaurus used to feed me Dandelion greens daily. They help me digest all my food."

"My mom roasts the Dandelion roots for herbal coffee." Nya added.

"And," squealed two little voices deep beneath their feet, "Dandelions are good for your garden! Their roots mine deep into the soil and bring up minerals and nutrients."

"That's right!" said Bronty to the friendly worms.

"Bronty, will you cook up some Dandelion greens for the big celebration? We'd love to try your GrannySaurus' recipe" the worms smiled.

"Sure thing," agreed Bronty. "See you there!"

CHAPTER 10: TWELVE HOURS LEFT

"BOO! BOO! BOO!"

Nya pointed, "Look at Franky Frog yelling at the plants."

"I'm trying to scare away all this Chickweed from my garden... BOO!" Franky yelled.

"Hey, I just noticed that Chickweed has a mohawk kind of like you," Nya said.

"That's how you can tell it's Chickweed," Bronty responded.

"Why don't you just eat it Franky?" Bronty asked. "I know it's just a weed, but it's also full of vitamins and minerals. It's tasty too!"

Franky wondered aloud, "It grows so fast. I'd need a party of dinosaurs to eat it all!"

"Lucky for you, that's where we're going," laughed Nya. "Why don't you harvest all this Chickweed and bring it to the celebration?"

"Yay! Great idea," Franky squealed in delight.

CHAPTER 11: SIX HOURS TO GO

Bronty was looking for two surprise treats before the big celebration started.

When Nya wasn't looking, he peered through the bushes until he found what he was looking for.

"Ah-ha! Ginger and Turmeric!" Bronty clapped.

He wrapped his tail around the Ginger stem and began to pull, but it wouldn't budge. Bronty gave another giant tug and finally... POP! Out came the root with Kimberlee Kimbetosalis attached.

"Oh! Hello there. I didn't see you picking the same plant," laughed Bronty.

"Hello, friend!" said a soil-crusted Kimberlee. "I wanted to collect some Turmeric for a cut on my paw. It's the perfect antiseptic."

"We can share," suggested Bronty. "I eat a little each day to keep me healthy. There's plenty for us and the celebration, too."

"Of course we can share." agreed Kimberlee. "And I can't wait for the party! I'll see you there soon."

CHAPTER 12: THE BIG CELEBRATION

It was finally the day of the big celebration.

"HAPPY BIRTHDAY, NYA!!" shouted everyone.

"I have a special surprise for you," said Bronty. "A magic salad filled with all the healing herbs we found this week."

"That's a wonderful present!" Nya danced with glee.

"Don't forget my super shiitake mushrooms!" Liam exclaimed. "They grew in just seven days. They're packed full of protein too, that makes them perfect for humongous herbivores like Bronty!"

"They're good for little humans, too." Bronty added as he proudly presented the special birthday salad to Nya.

She could see Shiitakes, Peppermint, Yarrow, Stinging Nettles, Elderberries, Pine Needles, Tulsi Basil, Plaintain, Passion Flowers, Chamomile, Dandelions, Chickweed, Ginger and Turmeric!

Can you find them too?

Made in the USA
Coppell, TX
21 December 2020